This book is a Junior
Library Guild Selection.

The Scary Wind
Hedgehog and Rabbit Collection

© Text: Pablo Albo, 2016
© Illustrations: Gómez, 2016
© Edition: NubeOcho, 2017
www.nubeocho.com – info@nubeocho.com

Original title: *El susto del viento*
Translator: Kim Griffin
Text editing: Ben Dawlatly and Rebecca Packard

Distributed in the United States by
Consortium Book Sales & Distribution

First edition: 2017
ISBN: 978-84-945971-7-6

Printed in China by Asia Pacific Offset,
respecting international labor standards.

Hedgehog and Rabbit

The Scary Wind

PABLO ALBO

ILLUSTRATED BY
GÓMEZ

nubeOCHO

Hedgehog and Rabbit were in the garden.
Rabbit was eating cabbages, and Hedgehog was
looking for snails.

The wind began to play with a pile of leaves,
and they swirled around in the air.

Rabbit became very frightened.
He screamed and hid in a
hollow tree trunk.

Hedgehog hadn't seen the swirling
leaves, but Rabbit's scream startled
him, so he followed Rabbit into the
log to see what was the matter.

"Oh! It was bigger than you and me together!

And it was filthy... full of dirt and dry leaves!

And it howled like the wind... OOOOHHHH!"

The wind kept blowing the leaves, and
some of them flew into the tree trunk
where Rabbit and Hedgehog were hiding.

"Oh no! Here it comes!" shouted Rabbit, and he ran out one end of the hollow log without looking back.

"Help!" yelled Hedgehog, who hadn't seen anything but was startled by Rabbit's commotion. He ran out the other end of the hollow log, all his quills standing on end.

Rabbit ran and ran. He was so, so frightened. His powerful legs took him far away very quickly.

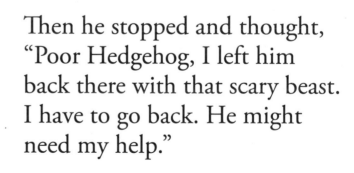

Then he stopped and thought, "Poor Hedgehog, I left him back there with that scary beast. I have to go back. He might need my help."

Rabbit decided to head back to the hollow tree trunk. On the way, he thought that he would look more fierce if he covered himself in mud. He also tied two big branches on his head that looked like horns.

Meanwhile, Hedgehog ran and ran until he found a hole to hide in.

Then he thought, "Poor Rabbit, he might be in danger."

Hedgehog decided to head back to the hollow tree trunk. On the way, he rolled in a pile of dry leaves so that they would stick to his quills. He also grabbed two big branches that looked like sharp claws.

Rabbit and Hedgehog got to the hollow tree trunk at the same time, each coming from a different direction.

Hedgehog didn't recognize Rabbit because he was covered in mud and he had two terrifying horns on his head.

"ROOOAARRR!" said Hedgehog to scare him away.

And, of course, Rabbit didn't recognize Hedgehog because of the leaves that were stuck to his quills and the branches that looked like claws.

"GRRRRRR!" said Rabbit to scare him away.

Hedgehog pulled off his fake claws and ran to the left, all his quills standing on end.

As he ran, the leaves that were stuck to his quills fell off one by one.

Rabbit threw off his false horns and ran off to the right, without looking back, frightened out of his wits.

The mud that was stuck to him plopped off with each leap.

Now, without his disguise, Rabbit got to
the other side of the garden and saw that
something was running toward him.

"Hedgehog! Thank heavens I found you! I thought that a monster with big claws had caught you. But don't worry, I think that we can make it back to the garden. I scared it away."

"Oh, Rabbit! I am so glad to see you! I thought that a beast with big horns had eaten you up. It is a good job that I frightened it off. I don't think that it will be back. I scared it to death."

So together they went back to the garden.

Rabbit went back to eating cabbages but kept looking out of the corner of his eye in case the beast returned.

Hedgehog got back to hunting for snails, keeping his ears pricked in case anything tried to sneak up on him.

The wind kept on stirring up the leaves and swirling the dust on the road, blowing everything farther away into the distance. Luckily for Hedgehog and Rabbit, the wind would not return to frighten them.